Silas Wood Hazeltine

The Traveller's Dream, and Other Poems

Silas Wood Hazeltine

The Traveller's Dream, and Other Poems

ISBN/EAN: 9783744707770

Printed in Europe, USA, Canada, Australia, Japan

Cover: Foto ©Andreas Hilbeck / pixelio.de

More available books at **www.hansebooks.com**

THE

TRAVELLER'S DREAM

AND

OTHER POEMS.

BY

SILAS WOOD HAZELTINE.

———•———

BOSTON:
PUBLISHED FOR THE AUTHOR.
1860.

To My Parents —

Who watched over my infancy, guided my youthful feet, and taught me the way of duty; who have always so kindly regarded my prefent and future welfare, and lavifhed upon me their love and kindness, — as a fmall token of gratitude, this volume is moft refpeftfully and affeftionately infcribed by their Son,

THE AUTHOR.

PREFACE.

—◆—

THE poems which compose this volume — if such they
may be called — are the youthful efforts of the author,
and as such they should be considered. The critic will
not expect the mountain-born stream to be a broad,
deep river in its early course; — or, in other words, he
will not look to find in these effusions either the per-
fectness of style or the depth of thought which marks
the matured poet, and which can only be acquired by few,
even after long years of apprenticeship to the Muses.
It is hoped, however, that their perusal will not be
entirely devoid of pleasure and benefit to those who have

> " a heart to feel
> The poetry and sacredness of things."

The piece entitled " The Sexton's Grave," was com-
posed at the age of fifteen, though the others were
mostly written from three to eight years later. The

greater part of them are here collected from various newspapers and magazines, to which they were originally contributed. Some ten or twelve, however, now appear in print for the first time. Many of them have been so extensively copied in the periodicals throughout the country, and have won such favorable notices and criticisms, from various sources, that the author is led to hope that he does not too rashly intrude in thus formally presenting himself to Mr. Public. He would hardly have taken such a step, had it not been for the encouragement and advice of several literary acquaintances, and the belief that he has many friends in all parts of the Union who will greet his humble volume with no unfriendly welcome.

CONTENTS.

	Page
THE TRAVELLER'S DREAM	17
MY FORTUNE	21
STANZAS	24
GONE TO DWELL IN HEAVEN	26
THIS WORLD IS BEAUTIFUL TO ME	29
I SAID I WOULD FORGET THEE	31
A REQUIEM	33
DEATH	35
"WHERE THERE'S A WILL, THERE IS A WAY"	36
JENNY DALE	38
LIFE AND DEATH	40
OH, CENSURE NOT YOUR BROTHER MAN	43
HAPPY THOUGHTS	45
DYING, PERCHANCE	46
A HYMN OF THANKS	48
ALBUM TRIBUTE	49
I WOULD NOT CALL THEE MINE	51

DEPARTED GENIUS 53

THE BITTEREST CUP 55

NEVER COURT BUT ONE 57

THE GIRLS WE LOVE THE BEST 60

PROSPERITY AND ADVERSITY 61

OUR PARTING. — TO NETTIE 63

MY BROTHER'S GRAVE 66

"CAST THY BREAD UPON THE WATERS" . . . 68

EVA MOORE 70

THE COT AND THE MILL 72

THE PLAIN TRUTH 74

ALL ALONE TO-DAY I WANDER 77

WARP AND WOOF 79

THE BRIDE 81

EVEN 85

DISEASE 87

REVELATION 89

WE MET 92

"I CANNOT DO IT" 95

SORROW 97

HE BUT CAME HOME TO DIE 99

THE HEART THAT HAS LOVED 102

THE SONGS OF THE DEAD 104

UPWARD AND ONWARD 106

ANGELS 109

THOU SAY'ST A HAPPY LIFE IS THINE . . . 112

WELL, THERE! IF IT DOES N'T BEAT ALL . . 114

THE EYES 116

TO ———— 117

WRATH 119

CAN I FORGET THEE ? 120

THE SEXTON'S GRAVE 122

FOR ANNETTE'S ALBUM 124

OUR CHILDHOOD'S HOME 125

THE SEPARATION 127

HAD THAT STAR SHONE FOR ME 131

SUMMER MORNING IN THE COUNTRY . . . 133

COME TO MY GRAVE, AND SMILE 135

WEEP NOT FOR HIM 137

REQUITED LOVE 139

THE LAKE OF YOUTH 141

TO A SISTER, WITH A PRESENT 144

MARINTHA 145

THE MAGDALEN 147

PARTING WORDS 149

WILT THOU REMEMBER ME? 151

STANZA 152

THE TRAVELLER'S DREAM.

THE TRAVELLER'S DREAM

SLEEP came and closed the trav'ler's eyes
  Far from his native shore,
And in his dreams he was at home
  With those he loved once more;
And kindred voices fell upon his ear,
In accents soothing, and in ·tones of cheer.

He stood at his own cottage-door,
  And saw the flowers around,
And the bright streamlet, as it passed,
  With its familiar sound;
And caught his ear the music of the breeze,
As it passed gently through the old roof-trees.

The honeysuckle's breath, it seemed
  To sweeten all the air,
And the dear homestead wore a smile,
  Such as it used to wear;
And sweet smiles played upon the sleeper's face,
As in his dreams he saw his native place.

And dreamed he that he sat again
  By his own cherished hearth,
And children that seemed unto him
  The loveliest on earth—
Because they were his own, clung to his knee,
And prattled to him in their childish glee.

And then again, as thus he dreamed,
  The sleeping trav'ler smiled,
And his hand moved as if to twirl
  The ringlets of a child;
And his lips moved as if a kiss to press
Upon some brow of infant loveliness.

And more than this, the trav'ler dreamed
  Of one far dearer still;

Of her who at the altar vowed
  To be his own until
Their souls should taste of everlasting life,
The mother of his darling babes, his wife.

Sleep took her weight from off his eyes,
  The traveller awoke;
He was a wanderer again,
  The blissful dream was broke!
"I was so happy," sighed he, "while I slept,"
Far from his home and all he loved, *he wept.*

The stars looked down upon his grief,
  Stars of a foreign sky,
And they, but the broad waste, were all
  That heard the trav'ler's cry.
No wonder that he wept; their light
Told him of eyes that used to shine as bright!

"Alas!" he cried, "this is the meed
  The traveller receives,
To pine for rest in that loved home
  Which far behind he leaves;

To only taste such bliss in dreams, and then
To wake and be a wanderer again!

" My heart wings over waste and wave
   With the quick speed of thought,
For I have found the trav'ler's views
   Are all too dearly bought!
I've gazed on many a ruined town and pile —
What sacrificed for it? alas! home's smile."

MY FORTUNE.

Who said the future no one knows?
　　The thought is false as it is old;
I know the very day I'll die —
　　I've been and had my fortune told!

I know, too, when and whom I'll wed;
　　I'll meet my wife within a year;
A farmer's daughter she, and lives
　　Not more than twenty miles from here.

I know, although we've never met,
　　These are the looks that she doth wear —
Sharp features, peaked nose and chin,
　　A freckled face, red eyes and hair!

Our married life will be all smooth,
  No sorrows will obscure the way —
But oh my bonny bride must die !
  One year, just, from our wedding day.

Then hope and joy will shed no light,
  No more I'll feel but grief and pain;
My heart will be a sepulchre,
  And I shall never wed again.

I almost wish I *did n't* know
  Just what the future is to be;
It makes me sad to think that death
  So soon *must* part my wife and me !

That I had never seen the hag
  Who thus my future path revealed,
Showing the thorns and brambles there,
  Which God in wisdom had concealed.

For, knowing now what is to come,
  When drinking of the cup of bliss,

'T will mar the sweetness of the taste
  To think, "there are dregs of woe in this!"

And when my fiftieth birthday nears—
  That is the time I am to die—
I fear my soul will cling to earth,
  And dread to feel that death is nigh.

Therefore, I wish I *did n't* know
  Just what the future is to be—
That I had not a chance to dread
  The sorrows which it hath for me!

STANZAS.

Oh! let me die in the calm, still night,
When the lamps of heaven are burning bright;
When the moon's sweet smile, over hill and dell,
Rests softly down with a magic spell;
For from childhood's morn, it has been my delight
To commune with those silent orbs at night.
And many a lesson they've taught my mind,
Of faith in the Being all-wise and kind.

I never yet gazed on the heavens afar,
Of a cloudless night, but each twinkling star
Looked down on me with an angel's smile,
Which said, "Weary mortals, a little while,
A little while longer to suffer below,
A few more days of trouble and woe,
Of struggling against temptation and sin,
And heaven's bright gate ye shall enter in!"

And it seems to me, when I gaze on high,
And see those bright worlds shining thick in the sky,
That they *must* have been made for an end more wise,
Than to dazzle and please our mortal eyes.
It seems to me that when life ends here,
And the soul finds wings in another sphere,
It has only to wish, through the endless air,
To fly to some star, and it shall be there!

Then let me die in the calm, still night,
When the lamps of heaven are burning bright!
Draw my dying couch to the window nigh,
And let me gaze up in the starry sky,
So I shall not think of the grave's dark bed,
But of brighter worlds where I soon shall tread;
And if fears arise, it will set them at rest,
And make the death-angel a pleasant guest!

GONE TO DWELL IN HEAVEN.

DEATH has claimed our little Corrie,
  Set his signet on her brow,
And her cheeks that were like cherries,
  Are as pale as marble now!
We have robed her in white garments,
  Pure and spotless, for the grave,
And one little golden ringlet
  Is the most that we can save!

We have crossed her white hands meekly
  O'er her little pulseless breast,
And they soon will lay her lowly
  'Neath the churchyard sod to rest!

And we've closed her eyelids gently
　O'er the dim and glassy eyes,
For the soul that gave them brightness
　Now has soared beyond the skies!

Yes, beyond the sky — to heaven,
　Our dear darling's soul hath fled;
Tell me not that she has perished,
　Tell me not that she is dead;
For I know that she is *living*
　Where the happy angels dwell;
It is but her spirit's clay-house
　We must lay down in the dell.

Yes, she's gone to dwell in heaven,
　Little Corrie, loved and fair,
And no more shall we behold her
　Till we go to meet her there.
Through our weary, weary journey,
　O'er this sorrow-clouded shore,
We shall never see the smiling
　Of her sweet face any more!

But when life on earth is over,
    In our Father's dwelling-place,
We will gaze again with rapture
    On our little Corrie's face!
There we'll press her to our bosoms,
    And will kiss her cheeks once more,
And, with hand in hand, forever
    We will roam the spirit-shore!

THIS WORLD IS BEAUTIFUL TO ME.

This world is beautiful to me,
　　This beautiful world of ours,
With grassy carpet, soft and green,
　　Figured with brilliant flowers;
And trees that break the outline rough,
　　Of hill and vale and sky,
Making them all in softness blend,
　　As light and shade o'erlie.

This world is beautiful to me,
　　With silver streams that sweep
So broadly, proudly, stately on,
　　To marry with the deep;
And over all tho arching sky,
　　Tinted so softly blue,
Where sunset paints the fleecy clouds
　　With such a gorgeous hue!

This world is beautiful to me,
　　And never do I gaze
Upon the blooming landscape round,
　　But what I feel to praise
The Infinitely Wise, who made
　　This world of ours so bright,
And gave, beside all that we need,
　　All that can please the sight.

And if a world more beautiful
　　Than this above is seen,
O'ercanopied and carpeted
　　With softer blue and green,
I scarce would dare to fly to it,
　　So dazzling it must be;
Oh, this delightful world of ours
　　Is fair enough for me!

I SAID I WOULD FORGET THEE.

I SAID I would forget thee,
  I said I would forget
How much my heart was given
  Into thy keeping yet;
And then I would be happy
  As if I'd loved thee not;
Long years since then have vanished,
  But thou art not forgot!

I said I would forget thee,
  And with heart light and free,
Join once more with the merry,
  In halls of revelry;

And in the lordly mansion,
And in the lowly cot,
I 've joined in mirth and revel,
But thou art not forgot!

In vain has been the conflict —
The struggle to forget
The songs which thou hast sung me,
The hours that we have met;
And till my heart, which throbbeth
For thee alone, beats not —
Till it is hushed forever,
Thou canst not be forgot!

A REQUIEM.

REST, brother, rest! no more wilt thou be weary,
  Thy hands no more will labor here with ours;
For thou hast found that land that grows not dreary,
    Where fade not flowers!

Rest, brother, rest! rest evermore from sorrow,
  Rest evermore from pain and sin and care;
Where life is one long day that brings no morrow,
    Rest, brother, there!

Rest, brother, rest! thy feet no more forever
  Shall roam the thorny path which thou hast trod;
Where life, and joy, and pleasure endeth never,
    Rest thee with God!

Rest, brother, rest! thine eyes have ceased from weeping,
   Thine ears have ceased discordant sounds to hear:
Where grief no more her lonely watch is keeping,
      Rest, loved and dear.

Rest, brother, rest! the burning tears we shower
   Upon the sod that lies upon thy breast,
Thou heedest not; nor hath the whole world power
      To break thy rest.

Rest, brother, rest! how often shall we miss thee,
   When we are gathered round the ingle-flame:
How oft in vain the lips that used to kiss thee,
      Shall call thy name!

And oh! how oft we'll long for that bright hour,
   When God shall raise the screen 'tween us and heaven,
That we may fly to meet where no more power
      To Death is given.

Rest, brother, rest! we're coming soon to meet thee
   In that bright world where thou art so much blest:
Gloom *must* hang o'er our hearts till there we greet thee ;
      Rest, brother, rest!

DEATH.

DEATH's step is soft; and when we little think
That such a monster can be creeping by,
We stand upon the grave's dark, awful brink,
And know nôt that our journey's end is nigh.

As trees that might see ages pass away,
At once are shattered by the lightning's blow,
E'en thus, when least expected, death may lay
The strong, the healthful and the blooming low.

Then, mortal man, so live from day to day,
That Death — come when or how he will — may
find
Thee ready and prepared to go away
To realms beyond the grave, unknown to mortal
mind.

"WHERE THERE'S A WILL, THERE IS A WAY."

Ye youth whose hearts are beating high,
  With longings for the battle strife, —
Who for the heated contest sigh,
  The contest in the field of life, —
Go forth with patience in your mood,
  Though hope's light giveth scarce a ray,
Remembering that old adage good,
  Where there's a will, there is a way.

Though many troubles hang around,
  Or in the path before ye lie,
With courage go, and they'll be found,
  As ye approach, to rise and fly.
And unto what Despondency,
  Or trembling Fear, or Doubt may say,
Reply, "I will not list to ye!"
  Where there's a will, there is a way.

And if you 're asked what failing means,
  Or what it is to cease to try,
Crowd to your eyes their fiercest beams,
  And answer, that it means to die!
As failing, there is no such thing,
  If ye but strive, and watch, and pray, —
If ye go forth remembering
  Where there 's a will, there is a way.

Go thus, hot youth! to battle, go, —
  Your longings are not all in vain;
But if ye firmly meet the foe,
  The victory ye 'll surely gain!
And unto what Despondency,
  Or trembling Fear, or Doubt may say,
Reply, " I will not list to ye!"
  Where there 's a will, there is a way!

JENNY DALE.

BENEATH the churchyard turf and flowers,
　All cold, and still, and pale,
Lies one I loved in by-gone hours,
　The fair young Jenny Dale!

She died ere scarce a shade of care
　Had touched her little heart, —
She knew not what it was, to bear
　Affliction's painful smart.

And now the wild birds come and sing
　Above her little grave;
The breezes there their music bring,
　And wild flowers o'er her wave.

And I am often there alone,
　To think of her and weep;

And there the low winds seem to moan,
"Why did'st thou fall asleep?"

Yet I would not recall her form
   From yon bright land of bliss,
To brave again life's wintry storm,
   In such a world as this.

No! let her dwell on that bright shore,
   From every sorrow free;
I would not have her come once more,
   To tread life's path with me.

For she is happier there, I know,
   Where bright-winged angels dwell,
Than I could make her here below;
   Sweet Jenny Dale, farewell!

O sleep, sleep on, my Jenny dear,
   Beneath the flowery sod;
Though sadly do I miss thee here,
   Soon we shall meet with God.

LIFE AND DEATH.

This life is but a day, a fleeting day,
Spent at the doorstead of eternity;
For earth is but the portal of that fair
And glorious mansion where our Father dwells.
We linger on the door-step for awhile,
A few short, precious hours — and this is life!
And then we take a step, a little step
Across the threshold of the house, to dwell
Forever more within — and this is death!

Yet, transient as it is, this life was not
By God bestowed upon us all in vain.
Oh, no; the time allotted us on earth
Is given to us for great purposes.

Not to win honor, titles, power, wealth,
Or we could take them with us through the door;
But to win all that we can carry hence —
The treasures of the soul. 'T is given us
That we might better be prepared for heaven,
By tasting life as it is here — this life
Of pain and sorrow. Only thus could we
Eternal bliss learn to appreciate.
And it is given us to train the mind,
The immortal soul that never dies — that we,
When our probation shall be ended here,
May enter heaven with germinated soul,
Prepared to grow in that immortal clime.

Then labor well thy mission to fulfil,
Lest you should go and leave it all undone.
Oh, think that life is but a fleeting day, —
That you are e'en now standing at the door
Which opens into heaven! Only one step
To your eternal home! and oh! that step
May soon be taken, none can tell how soon.
To-morrow, or perhaps to-day will be
The last day you shall linger here on earth;

And but a little while, at most, we know,
Is given us to do our labor here.
Oh, then, at any time be thou prepared,
Frail man, to take *the involuntary step*
Across the threshold of eternity !

OH, CENSURE NOT YOUR BROTHER MAN.

Oh, CENSURE not your brother man
  Because of his belief;
A voice has reached his ear, perchance,
  To which your own was deaf.
And many a tenet may be true,
Although it seemeth wrong to you.

A strain of music over you
  May have a charming spell,
While some may hear no sweetness in't,
  Or love it not so well.
Their ears were never made to hear
The strains you think so sweet and clear.

A little flower to you may seem
  Most beautiful and sweet,

While others, to its beauty blind,
  Would crush it 'neath their feet.
Their eyes were never made to view
The beauty that's revealed to you.

You cannot reach all hearts the same,
  Whate'er your skill or tact;
For God made not his children all,
  Alike to think and act.
What gives one joy and happiness,
May give another pain, distress.

Then censure not your brother man
  Because of his belief;
A voice has reached his ear, perchance,
  To which your own was deaf.
And many a tenet may be true,
Although it seemeth wrong to you.

HAPPY THOUGHTS.

How full the thoughts of pleasure
    That when this life is o'er,
Each lovely human treasure
    That is ours on earth no more,   .
We shall meet again in heaven,
   Where they never, never die;
That eternity shall measure
    That meeting in the sky!

And how full the thoughts of pleasure,
    That when we meet them there,
We'll be safely moored forever
    Beyond the reach of care;
That our hearts shall know no longer
    Sorrow, suffering or fear,
And our path be one of flowers,
    Through the never-ending year!

DYING, PERCHANCE.

O'ER the long space that parts us, mother,
  Would I could fly to-day,
To cheer thy fond and loving heart,
  And drive thy pain away;
For thou art on a bed of pain,
  Disease hath bleached thy brow,
And while I roam so far away,
  Perchance thou'rt dying now!

Dying, perchance — oh! mad'ning thought —
  I *must* fly unto thee!
What if the lips that taught mine own
  Should speak no more to me! —

The robin on my window-bough
  His blithesome matin sings;
He knows not how he pains my heart—
  Hush, bird! lend me thy wings!

Nay, fly thou! for some swifter way
  My mad'ning heart must find,
Oh! give me wings to fly like light,
  Or thought across the mind!
Nay, swifter! these are all too slow!
  As prayer speeds up above,
So, mother! would I fly to thee,
  And heal thee with my love!

A HYMN OF THANKS.

O THOU great God, whose mighty power
    Hath filled the sky with countless spheres,
To thee I bring for this glad hour
    An offering of grateful tears.

And those which now suffuse my eyes,
    Thou know'st are but a little part
Of the deep fountain whence they rise,
    The fulness of my thankful heart.

My bosom sea grew dark and rough,
    Within how fearful was the night!
I cannot thank thee, Lord, enough
    For making it so calm and bright.

Accept the tribute which I bring
    For thy kind mercy here below,
And teach me sweeter praise to sing,
    And deeper love for thee to know.

ALBUM TRIBUTE.

I ASK not friend, (because 'tis vain)
   Joy o'er thy path may always shine;
Pleasure on earth is mixed with pain,
   And such a cup, I know, is thine.
All I would ask is this: that He
   Who gives the bitter and the sweet,
May give thee strength, when pleasures flee,
   Life's cold and adverse storms to meet.

Oh, it is kindness in our God,
   While exiled here on earth we roam,
To chasten sometimes with his rod,
   To tell us this is not our home;

To make us look beyond this life,
  To that bright realm of endless day,
Where all unknown are care and strife,
  And joy and hope fade not away!

Then do not, friend, bow down thy head —
  When sorrow cometh — to the dust;
But lift thine eyes — though joy hath fled —
  Above, with still unfaltering trust;
And pray, though hope seems not to live,
  A brighter day will soon be given;
So shall e'en grief some pleasure give,
  And thou shalt learn the way to Heaven.

I WOULD NOT CALL THEE MINE.

FAREWELL! thy hand I would not take,
   Unless the gift contained thy heart;
Far better for each other's sake,
   To wear life's galling chain apart.
I love thee, worship thee! but still,
   If deep within that heart of thine,
My passion wakes no answering thrill,
   I would not wish to call thee mine!

Without thee, life will be a waste,
   My heart of every pleasure void,—
E'en bliss, though offered to the taste,
   Without thee cannot be enjoyed.

But since my love availeth not,
  Doth in thy soul no echo wake,
I would not have thee share my lot—
  Oh, better that my heart should break!

Farewell! though it is death to part;
  Farewell! 'tis more than death to me;
I cannot teach my self-willed heart,
  To beat for any one but thee!
And yet, though doomed to love thee still,
  Since deep within that heart of thine,
My passion wakes no answering thrill,
  I would not wish to call thee mine!

DEPARTED GENIUS.

EARTH! from thy sphere is taken
A mind that beamed with genius' brilliant rays;
A spirit filled with a mysterious light,
Which made this mortal shore more fair and bright;
A soul that could awaken
Strains to enchant the world, and win its glorious
praise.

His was the poet's vision:
To him the face of Nature wore no veil:
Where, unto others, was but deepest gloom,
He saw a lovely paradise in bloom,
And heard sweet tones Elysian,   .
Where others heard no sound except an earthly wail.

And his the magic power
To paint to mortals with the brush of thought,
The beauteous visions of the world on high,
Which Muse revealed unto his poet-eye; —

To give man precious dower,
In form of heavenly songs his ear from angels caught.

Weep, Earth! that he is taken
So soon away. Upon his noble brow
Time sat as lightly as untrodden snow,
That clothed the fields but one short hour ago;
Yet death's strong wind hath shaken
The young and blooming tree; it lieth prostrate now!

Kneel at your altars weeping,
Ye who with rapture gave his song an ear;
Go to your duties with a saddened heart,
That worth and genius should so soon depart;
So soon in death be sleeping—
That calm and stirless sleep, no more to charm us here.

Yet hoping that when riven
Are all the ties that bind us to this shore—
When Death's cold hand shall put our limbs in chains,
And freeze the blood now warm within our veins,
We may meet him in heaven,
And feel a joyous thrill to hear his song once more.

THE BITTEREST CUP.

Not the weeping mourner,
  Not the child of want;
Not the suffering martyr,
  The object of scorn and taunt;
Not the love-forsaken,
  Not the one who sups
Deep of disappointment,
  Drinketh the bitterest cup.

Not the ruined tradesman,
  Not the penniless;
Not the one whom Fortune
  Never turns to bless;
Not the one who, striving
  Fame's hill to go up,
Meeteth but repulses,
  Drinketh the bitterest cup.

Not the helpless orphan,
    Left on earth alone ;
Not the one who heareth
    Never friendship's tone ;
Not the one who suffers
    Painful, long disease,
Drinketh the cup most bitter —
    No, not such as these.

But the one whose conscience
    Feels the sting of crime,
And must feel its burden
    Through all coming time, —
He whose darkened bosom
    Ne'er shall be lighted up
By innocence or peace again,
    Drinketh the bitterest cup.

NEVER COURT BUT ONE.

I HAVE finished it,—the letter
  That will tell him he is free;
From this moment, and forever,
  He is nothing more to me!
And my heart feels lighter, gayer,
  Since the deed at last is done;
It will teach him that when courting,
  He should never court but one!

Everybody in the village
  Knows he's been a-wooing me,
And this morning he was riding
  With that saucy Anna Lee!

And they say he smiled upon her
   As he cantered by her side;—
I will warrant you he promised
   To make her soon his bride!

But I've finished it,—the letter;
   From this moment he is free—
He may have her if he wants her,
   If he loves her more than me.
He may go—it will not kill me—
   I would say the same, so there,
If I knew it would; for flirting—
   It is more than I can bear!

It is twilight, and the evening
   That he said he'd visit me;
But no doubt he's now with Anna—
   He may stay there, for all me!
And as true as I'm a-living,
   If he ever comes here more,
I will act as if we never,
   Never, never met before!

It is time he should be coming,
　And I wonder if he will?
If he does, I'll look so coldly —
　What's that shadow on the hill?
I declare, out in the twilight,
　There is some one coming near —
Can it be? — yes, 'tis his figure,
　Just as true as I am here!

Now, I almost wish I'd written
　Not to him that he was free,
For, perhaps, 'twas but a story
　That he rode with Anna Lee.
There! he's coming through the gateway,
　I will meet him at the door,
And I'll tell him still I love him —
　If he'll court Miss Lee no more!

THE GIRLS WE LOVE THE BEST.

AN IMPROMPTU.

HERE's health to the girls, the beautiful girls,
Who make the world so blest;—
Especially to those fair ones
Whom of all we love the best.
Without them, oh! who could be glad,
Or contented with their lot?
Even heaven itself, without the girls,
Would be a wretched spot!

Oh, bless the Lord that Adam's rib
Was ever taken out;
For we can all forget our cares,
If the girls are but about!
Their sunny smiles send light and warmth
To every heart and breast;
Then here's a health, a joyous health,
To the girls we love the best!

PROSPERITY AND ADVERSITY.

When the brilliant sun is shining
  O'er the hill, and o'er the lea;
When his rays are gayly dancing
  Everywhere, we do not see

Worlds and systems brightly gleaming,
  Twinkling in the distant blue;
But when day no more is beaming,
  Heaven seems opened to our view!

Thus with life; when joy and gladness
  Fill the overflowing heart;
When no forms of care and sadness
  In life's drama bear a part,—

We 're forgetful of the treasures
　Heaven upon us can bestow,
And think only of the pleasures
　We may here enjoy below.

But when storms of pain and sorrow
　Darkly shroud enjoyment's light;
When despair hangs o'er the morrow,
　And our way seems black as night;

Then we turn from earthly visions,
　To the fount of heavenly bliss,
And the soul looks from its prison
　To a brighter world than this!

OUR PARTING.—TO NETTIE.

I THOUGHT not when we parted
   At the little cottage door,
Such long, long years would vanish
   Before we met once more;
But I felt a strange, sad feeling,
   Which I did not understand,
As I said, "Good-by, dear Nettie,"
   And took your proffered hand.

To my eyes there came the teardrops,
   To my heart there came a pain,
But I knew not 'twas a boding
   That we should not meet again!

Now I know why 't was I lingered,
  Gazing sadly in your face,
As if within my heart-shrine,
  I would every feature trace.

Oh! even now I'm weeping
  To live that parting o'er,
For I wander back in fancy,
  And we're standing at the door;
And your hand again I'm pressing,
  And again I say, " Good-by,"
But I feel now we are parting
  Even for eternity!

It is o'er; again we've parted,
  And upon life's dreary main,
Far apart our barks are drifting,
  To never meet again;
But the same bright haven, Nettie,
  Shall be ours, I know, at last —
I shall meet thee, I shall meet thee,
  When this dreary main is past!

Dost remember how in childhood
   I gathered flowers for thee?
Unfading ones I'll bring thee
   Where our meeting next shall be!
'T will be where there is no parting,
   Where we no more shall sigh;
And till then, my dear friend Nettie,
   Till then, good-by, good-by!

MY BROTHER'S GRAVE.

Do you know the spot where my brother sleeps?
Have you seen the willow that o'er him weeps?
'Tis a lovely spot, and it is my prayer,
And my wish, kind friends, to be buried there.
I remember how, in the days gone by,
All my sadness would flee when his form came nigh;
But alas! death came, and he passed away,
Like the shades of twilight at close of day.
And now he sleeps 'neath the willow tree,
And there, kind friends, you must bury me.

Oh! sacred to me is that little mound
Where my brother sleeps, in the churchyard-ground;
And I wander oft when the night draws near,
To water its dust with the bitter tear;

Yet I'd not recall to this tainted earth,
His spirit to dwell by our fireside-hearth;
For I know he's gone to a brighter shore,
Where the soul may rest, and they weep no more;
And where — sweet to think — when this life is past,
To part no more, we shall meet at last.

Ah me! how my heart bows down with woe,
When, as twilight falls o'er his grave, I go
And sit there under the willow tree,
That bends o'er the headstone mournfully,
To think of the days that will ne'er come back,
And of him who has fled from life's thorny track!
But I love to think that when life is past,
I shall come and lie by his side at last;
Then remember it is my fervent prayer,
And my wish, kind friends, to be buried there!

"CAST THY BREAD UPON THE WATERS."

Cast thy bread upon the waters,
  · And it will not be in vain;
God will note the act of kindness,
  And return it all again.
Yes, when thou, perchance, dost need it,
  He'll return it triple-fold;
And the joy such deeds will bring thee —
  It can never half be told.

Cast thy bread upon the waters,
  And the glorious Giver praise;
For he will return it to thee,
  " After many, many days."

God will bless the man who giveth
  To the needy and the poor,
And who to the helpless orphan,
  Opens wide his heart and door.

Though thy treasure be but little,
  Of that little give a part;
Heaven will look not on its value,
  But the motive in thy heart.
Cast thy bread upon the waters,
  And it will not be in vain;
God will note the act of kindness,
  And return it all again.

EVA MOORE.

In the garden bower was sitting
   Eva Moore, and by her side
Allan Gray, who on the morrow
   Was to claim her as his bride.
Said he, "Shall we not be happy,
   Shall we not be happy, sweet?
Time will only scatter flowers,
   Thornless flowers beneath our feet."

And she answered, "Oh, so happy,
   Folded in each other's love;
All our life will seem a foretaste
   Of a brighter one above!"

Oh! 't was well that happy Eva
  Could not ope the future's door,
And behold how soon her pathway
  Was to be all clouded o'er.

Since the eve they sat together
  In the bower a year hath fled,
And poor Eva Moore is weeping,
  For her Allan lieth dead!
One short year they have been happy,
  "Folded in each other's love;"
Now their paths by fate are severed,
  One below and one above.

Such is life; the happy bridal
  Oft is near the mournful tomb;
And the brightest hour of pleasure,
  Near the darkest hour of gloom;
But 't is wise and kind in Heaven,
  That we cannot ope the door,
And behold, far in the future,
  Where the clouds must gather o'er!

THE COT AND THE MILL.

HAVE you seen the cot and the old gray mill,
That stand at the foot of a rock-ribbed hill?
Have you seen the poplars towering high,
On the banks of the river which wanders by?
Have you seen the dam where the waters pour?
And the garden and lawn before the door?
That beautiful spot is my childhood's home,
And I'll cherish it still, wherever I roam.

There I have planted and watched with care
Sweet flowers that scented the summer air;
There I have roamed in sweet, childish glee,
With playmates dear, over hill and lea;

There I was wont in my youth to rejoice
At my mother's smile, and my father's voice ;
And there (alas ! we shall meet no more,)
With my brothers I played on the lawn at the door !

Far, far from that spot I roam to-day,
Where the breezes of summer forever play ;
Where the trees are covered with tropical bloom,
And the air is laden with sweet perfume ;
But my heart wings over the waste between,
And fondly broods down o'er that cherished scene.
And I never shall cease to love that spot,
Till the time shall come when my heart beats not !

THE PLAIN TRUTH.

You watch your neighbor's actions
    More than you do your own;
You cannot, or you will not,
    Let his affairs alone!
In short, your neighbor's business,
    Which none concerneth you,
You meddle with till yours
    Is wholly out of view!

You see your neighbor's failings,
    But cannot see your own,
And think that you are worthy
    To cast at him the stone;

But if you'd wipe your mirror
   Till you yourself could see,
You'd find you're quite as erring,
   And full of faults as he.

The way you judge a person,
   Is by the cloth he wears;
You never stop to notice
   The inward heart he bears;
But if his dress is seedy,
   Or growing old and torn,
You pass him by unnoticed,
   Or look at him with scorn.

But if he has fine garments,
   And wears a golden chain,
You hesitate no longer
   That person to ordain
A gentleman; you praise him,
   You laud him to the skies;—
No matter, if he *dresses*,
   If he isn't good and wise!

You feel yourself above those
  Not quite so rich as you
Too proud to call him brother,·
  Whose hard-earned dimes are few.
But one word in your ear, sir,
  It may be, by and by —
For fortune's wheel keeps turning —
  You 'll be low and he be high!

ALL ALONE TO-DAY I WANDER.

ALL alone to-day I wander
  In the orchard — it is May,
And the apple-trees are blooming,
  And the earth is blithe and gay;
But my heart is full of sorrow,
  For 't was just a year ago
That I wandered here with Nelly,
  Who is in the grave so low!

.

Just a year — the apple-blossoms
  Scented all the air as now,
And I wove of them a chaplet
  For my darling Nelly's brow;

Then I gazed upon her beauty,
    Little thinking I should pray —
Weep and pray o'er dear lost Nelly,
    Long before another May!

But she died! the snows of winter
    Once have melted on her grave,
And the flowers we loved to gather,
    For the first time o'er her wave;
And the orchard-trees are covered
    With a dress of pink and white,
And again the May is smiling,
    And again the earth is bright!

And again I've sought the orchard,
    But my heart is full of woe,
For I think of her who wandered
    With me here a year ago;
And the trees with blossoms covered,
    The air filled with sweet perfume,
Only mind me of the beauty
    That lies faded in the ·tomb!

WARP AND WOOF.

LIFE hath trouble, life hath sorrow,
  Life hath suffering, pain and care,
Making oftentimes the morrow
  Seem too sad for us to bear.

Life hath joy, and life hath pleasure,
  Life hath even drops of bliss,
Making all beyond the azure
  Seem a larger type of this.

And of these an all-wise Heaven
  Weaveth every web of life;
Pleasure for the warp is given,
  Which must have its woof of strife

For if clouds were never o'er us,
  If joy never had its ebb,
Heaven would never seem before us,
  Life would be a woofless web.

Murmur not, then, when He weaveth
  In thy life-web threads of woe;
Should not He by whom man liveth,
  What is best for mortals know?

Who, when suffering is given,
  E'en in thought shall dare complain,
Knowing that an all-wise Heaven
  Weaveth in the threads of pain!

THE BRIDE.

'Twas the day before the bridal,
  Health her cheeks like roses dyed,
And her lips exclaimed "To-morrow
  I shall be a happy bride!
I shall stand before the altar
  With one dear to me as life,
And with heaven's benediction,
  I shall go away his wife.
I am happy, oh how happy!
  Sorrow never can betide —
It can never cloud my pathway,
  While my Charlie's by my side!"

It is morn, the bridal morning,
　And the dew is off the grass,
And an hour ago the bridegroom
　Came to claim his pretty lass.
But she cometh not to greet him,
　What can keep her thus away?
Surely she who loved him fondly,
　Will become his wife to-day?
Surely she who but last even
　Was so happy in her love,
And was longing for the bridal,
　Cannot now unfaithful prove?

Ah, poor Charlie! in your bosom
　Let the canker rankle deep;
You will never be her husband —
　You must go away and weep!
I'm aware 't was but last even
　That you lingered by her side,
Talking of the happy ·future,
　But she's now another's bride!

Weep! poor Charlie, for last midnight,
   God who gave your darling breath,
Sent an angel who persuaded
   Her to be the bride of Death!

Put that dress of snowy satin,
   And that bridal veil aside,
And a robe of spotless linen
   Put upon the new made bride!
Part the curls back from her forehead,
   Where last night a kiss was pressed,
And her icy hands cross meekly
   O'er the still and pulseless breast;
And a wreath of pure white lilies
   Put around the sleeper's head,
For the cold clay of the churchyard
   Is to be her bridal bed!

Now look at her as she lieth,
   For the deep, damp grave arrayed;
Never yet a look more peaceful
   Rested on a mortal maid!

Never bride was made more happy
  On her bridal morn than she!
And the smile her· lips still curling,
  Asks, "Why do you weep for me?"
There! you've laid her on her pillow,
  Where the birds sing all the day,—
You've performed the last kind service—
  She is happy, come away!

EVEN.

Oh! I love to stray at even,
    When the day has gone to sleep;
When upon the brow of heaven
    Stars their nightly vigils keep;
When the pale moon looks down calmly
    O'er the meadow and the lea;
For the quiet of the night-time
    Hath a pleasing charm for me.

Oh! I love to stray at even,
    In the dusky shades of night,
To think of the cherished blossoms
    That have faded from my sight;

Of the ones who grew a-weary
  On the toilsome march of life,
And unto the grave departed,
  Where there comes no care or strife.

Then the breezes seem to whisper,
  And the bright stars seem to say,
"Your departed friends are near you
  All the night and all the day;
They are near you, though you see not
  The bright gleaming of their eyes;
They are near to lead you upward
  To a home in Paradise."

DISEASE.

Disease is but an angel in disguise,
  Sent down by God, the spirit's prison-door
To ope and let it free, that to the skies,
  Its native place, it may return once more:

An angel, sent to wean the immortal soul,
  With throes of pain from this probative sphere,
That when we 've written o'er life's little scroll,
  We may not have a wish to linger here.

And were he driven from the homes of earth,
  Dark as it is, this world would be too bright,
And man would never wish for higher birth,
  To pass through death-gloom up to brighter light.

But when thy strong, throe-sending hand, Disease,
  Doth wrack our frame with pain and agony,
Earth hath no power our soul to hold and please,
  We long to soar to brighter realms on high.

Oh! kind it was in God who placed us here,
  To send us sick-bed agony and woe,
That when our freedom and a brighter sphere
  Is offered us, we might not cling below!

REVELATION.

This world a revelation is,
  With God's word written out
So legibly on every leaf
  We have no cause to doubt.
How can we gaze upon the sea,
  Or on the flowery sod,
Or on the sparkling sky at night,
  And read not, "There 's a God!"

I learn from every blade of grass,
  Of his almighty power;
And eyes that Nature's book can read,
  May see on every flower

The name of its great Maker, God,
 And his command to man,
" Love you your neighbor as yourself,
 Cheer all the hearts you can."

And he has written on his works,
 Around us and above,
On all his gifts for one and all,
 " There is a God of love."
And plainly as on printed page,
 Upon both land and sea,
I read in glowing characters,
 " Have thou no God but me."

But not alone in nature's writ
 Is God to us made known;
In the low wind he *speaks* to us,
 And in the thunder's tone;
And every voice, from the low chirp
 Of insects on the sod,
To the loud murmur of the sea,
 Cries out, " There is a God!"

This world a revelation is,
  With God's word written out
So legibly on every leaf
  We have no cause to doubt.
How can we gaze upon the sea,
  Or on the flowery sod,
Or on the sparkling sky at night,
  And read not, "There's a God!"

WE MET.

We met, but, meeting, not a smile
   Did either of us wear;
You might have read our features, but
   By the expression there,
Or by the few cold words we said —
   You would have called them such —
You 'd not have thought we e'er had loved,
   We who have loved so much!

I met his dark eye's piercing gaze,
   And every nerve I strung,
For fear that he would read my heart,
   With bitter anguish wrung;
For fear that he would see how well,
   How much I loved him yet,
When I would scorn to have him know
   I had the least regret!

All for the sake of pride I strove
  To wear a happy look,
As if I, too, was blest, as if
  My spirit was not shook.
And when a witty thing was said,
  I laughed against my will,
A happy laugh, to make him think
  I did not love him still!

And oh! he was deceived, I know,
  He must have thought me blest;
My looks did not betray the grief
  That rankled in my breast;
And when we came to part, my pride
  And firmness lingered yet,
And with an icy look and tone,
  · We parted as we met!

And now I'm in my room alone,
  But not deceiving now,
For all the anguish of my heart
  Is written on my brow!

My face no longer wears a mask
  Of looks all calm and cold,
And there is stain upon my cheeks,
  Where the tear-drops have rolled!

I'm thinking of the sunny past,
  When he was all to me;
Alas! in that respect, to-day
  Is just the same, I see!
And must it be so still, must I
  Still sigh, weep, and regret?
Oh, for one draught of Lethe's stream,
  That I, too, might forget!

My poor, weak heart, peace, peace! be still!
  Mourn not! why wilt thou sigh?
Be glad! it was not love he gave;
  Love doth not change or die.
He was unworthy of thy trust,
  Oh, give him not thy tears;
Be strong! and hopefully await
  The mede of future years!

I CANNOT DO IT.

"CANNOT do it?" yes you can, sir.
  Never say those words again;
But with perseverance try it,
  And you will not try in vain.
If at first you cannot conquer,
  Try again, and don't despair;
For there's none of us, poor mortals,
  Without some ill luck to bear!

Don't at trifles be discouraged,
  Work away with heart and hand;
Don't let disappointments daunt you,
  Don't be seen to idle stand;

For you 'll never conquer troubles,
    While in idleness you wait;
If you wish to be successful,
    Boldly meet the storms of fate!

Do not say, "I cannot do it"—
    These are words you should despise;
When one's heart is persevering,
    He will conquer, if he tries!
Then with energy and courage,
    Go to work, and never fear;
And how dark soe'er your troubles,
    You will see them disappear!

SORROW.

WHAT though the waves be rough,
  And life all wind and storm?
What though deep sorrow come,
  And cares in many a form!
What though our hopes all fade,
  And fortune bring us naught!
By lessons such as these,
  Must our blind souls be taught!

If always shone the sun
  Upon the fair green earth,
'Twould be a desert vast,
  Where nothing could have birth.

And thus, if o'er the soul
  Were ever sunny skies,
'Twould be a desert too,
  Where nothing green could rise!

Oh! drink, and murmur not,
  Thy brimming cup of woes;
Without the rain and storm,
  How could we have the rose?
The petals of thy soul
  May need the rain, so cold;
For by the storm, alike
  The rose and soul unfold!

HE BUT CAME HOME TO DIE.

They laid him in the grave to-day,—
I saw them lay him there,
Then turned with breaking heart away,
O'erburdened with despair.
Long years he hath a wanderer been
Upon a distant shore,
And now, although but just returned,
He dwells on earth no more!
It seems as if the sun at noon
Had vanished from the sky;
For brother who hath just returned—
He but came home to die!

He wrote us from that far-off land
That he should soon come home,
To view again the cherished scenes
Where once he loved to roam.
Oh, joyful news! it filled my heart
With purest, sweetest joy,
But never once thought I that death
Would all our bliss destroy.
And ere he came, how very slow
The sluggish days moved by;
Ah, little thought I then that he
Was coming home to die!

He came at last! what bliss was mine
To clasp again his hand,
And welcome him with tears of joy
To his dear native land;
To meet once more his love-lit eye —
E'en now I see his look —
And hath he passed forc'er away?
The thought I cannot brook!

Alas! we scarce had welcomed him,
  Before we saw him lie
With death's pale seal upon his brow —
  He but came home to die!

Yet solacing it is, to think
  'Twas not a stranger's hand
His dying pillow smoothed for him,
  His burning forehead fanned;
That we through the long nights of pain
  Could watch beside his bed,
And, in the hour of parting, hear
  The last words that he said!
So, though our brimming cup of bliss
  Is turned to agony,
Thank God our brother dear was spared
  To reach his home to die!

THE HEART THAT HAS LOVED.

UNTO the heart that once hath loved,
  Truly, but oh! in vain,
A joy so sweet—a love so pure—
  Can never come again!
But o'er life's sky, like a midnight cloud,
  The years shall darkly pass,
And love's warm rays shall shine no more
  On the ruined heart—alas!

The wreck within may be hid with smiles,
  Which are ever bright and bland,
But 'tis like the ivy's verdancy
  That covers a ruin grand!

And think not, though the eyes are bright,
  Though the checks may wear no stain,
That the love-lorn heart is all restored —
  It can never love again!

There is a "love" which is not love,
  But something far more base;
Which lives on wealth and station high,
  Fair form, or charming face:
But where two souls together run,
  Like fallen drops of rain,
Woe, woe is theirs, if they must part, —
  They can never love again!

THE songs that were sung by the dead,
  Oh, never sing them now;
They open wounds that oft have bled,
  And pain the heart and brow!
The struggling tears o'erflow their bounds
  To hear those songs once dear,
For now they are but doleful sounds
  To strike the mourner's ear.
And voices that regard the pain
  Another's heart may know,
Should never sing those songs again
  To mourners here below.

The songs that were sung by the dead,—
    Oh, let them be forgot;
They turn the heart to the loved ones fled,
    And it grieves to see them not!
They can but draw the memory back
    To days forever o'er,
And make us tread the Past's dark track
    In misery once more.
And voices that regard the pain
    Another's heart may know,
Should never sing those songs again
    To mourners here below!

UPWARD AND ONWARD.

UPWARD — onward! never weary
  In the path thou shouldst pursue ;
Though thy sky be cloudy, dreary,
  Sunny smiles will soon break through.
If thou art but persevering,
  Thou wilt conquer all at last;
Then look upward, never fearing,
  Onward! though the storm falls fast.

Sometimes comes a day of sorrow,
  Sometimes comes a night of pain;
Never mind, perhaps to-morrow
  Life will be all bright again.

And in vain is harsh repining,
  Or a tear, or groan, or sigh;
Though the sun hath ceased its shining,
  Hope should yet illume the sky.

What though troubles you encounter?
  Care is known by every one;
Upward, onward! nerve thee stouter,
  And the storm will soon be done.
Frowns will not make burdens lighter,
  Neither make thy heart more gay;
Think the sun may shine the brighter,
  When the storm has passed away.

Upward—onward! let this ever
  Be thy watchword here below,
And whatever fate betide thee,
  Thou wilt conquer all, I know.
For the heart that's persevering
  Never yet was known to fail;
Then, though adverse winds assail thee,
  Do not sit down to bewail.

But be hopeful, and remember
That the darkest hour of night
Is the last before the morning
Comes with soft and dewy light.
Upward — onward! Perseverance
Will be master in the end;
And though enemies assail thee,
He will make them all to bend!

ANGELS.

ANGELS e'er attend
  On our footsteps here,
Though their silent wings
  We may never hear.
They are ever with us
  All the night and day,
Guarding us from danger,
  Lighting our dark way.

When our lips are parched
  With the fever's glow,
Silently their wings
  Fan our burning brow;

And their gentle fingers,
  Driving pain away,
Though we may not feel them,
  O'er our temples stray.

When our hearts are sad,
  When we shed the tear,
To bear up and soothe,
  They are ever near;
When within our bosoms
  Hope and pleasure die,
Our sad hearts to gladden,
  They are ever by.

And whene'er with sin
  We our hearts would stain,
They, to virtue's path,
  Call us back again;
And their "still small voices"
  Whisper in our ear,
"It will bring thee anguish,
  Sin not, brother dear!"

And when we, at last,
 On the bed of death,
Unto God who gave,
 Yield the parting breath,
With delight unbounded,
 They are hovering o'er,
To take back the exile
 To its native shore!

THOU say'st a happy life is thine,
  And I rejoice to think it so,
Though it reminds me of the joy
  I hoped for, but can never know;
Though it uncovereth a past
  That bringeth but regrets to me,
For oh, it was more brightly fair
  Than e'er my future lot can be!

Thou say'st thou'rt blest in every tie,
  And that thy heart is blithe and free;
How sadly comes the painful thought
  That such joy might have been for me!

Yet I rejoice to think a path
  Of happiness and peace is thine;
I would not have thy spirit feel
  The lonely wretchedness of mine.

Oh! even as the torch went out,
  Which Hope had trimmed for many a day,
My heart was full of deepest prayer
  That Heaven would bless thy earthly way;
Though since that hour, through midnight gloom,
  Few rays have bid me joy again,
Thank God that my fond prayers for thee
  Have not been heard by him in vain!

WELL, THERE! IF IT DOES N'T BEAT ALL.

WELL, there! if it does n't beat all
    That I e'er before heard in my life!
"Uncle John," who is eighty years old,
    At last he has got him a wife!
And how old, do you think, is the bride?
    You "guess between three and fourscore!"
Ho, ho! she is only sixteen, —
    A girl of sixteen, and no more!

Her locks hang in raven-hued curls,
    And her brow is unwrinkled and fair,
While he is all furrowed with age,
    And like snow is the shade of his hair.

And when they go by in the street,
   It causes a great deal of sport,
To see the old man lean on her,
   When she should have him for support.

If you'd seen them to-day as they passed,
   In spite of yourself you'd have smiled;
I declare she looked most young enough
   To be his great-granddaughter's child!
And the people all think it is strange
   She should marry an old man like him,
Who is wrinkled, and withered, and feels
   Old age in his every limb!

But to me it is not at all strange,
   For a million of gold is his name,
And the girls would be few, with a chance,
   Who would not do exactly the same!
He can't live much longer, you know,
   He's so withered, and feeble, and old,
And when he is dead and laid out of the way,
   She can have what she married, — his gold!

THE EYES.

I CARE not whether the eyes are black,
  Or whether they're gray or blue,
If they give but a sign of a loving heart,
  And one that is always true.
If affection's light is in its gleam,
  That eye is the eye for me;
I'll turn from all others to catch its ray,
  Whatever its hue may be.

Though bright the eye as the evening star
  On the azure brow of night,
It gives but a cold and chilling ray,
  If not lit with affection's light.
Then though poets may praise the soft blue eye,
  And others admire the black,
The eye for me is the one that gives
  An answering love-gleam back.

TO ———.

Not less bright than the stars that shine,
Lady, are those fair orbs of thine;
And in their depth, as in a glass,
Are mirrored the thoughts o'er thy soul that pass.

White thy brow as the virgin snow,
Smooth as a silent stream,—and oh !
Not less bright than the opening rose,
The bloom that doth on thy cheek repose.

Glossy as silk, thy nutbrown hair,
Never were curls more soft and fair;
And when thy lip with a smile is curled,
There's nothing more sweet in all the world.

Perfect the Artist thy form hath made,
Beauty is thine of the highest grade;
Every action is one of grace, —
Thou art an angel in form and face!

But not for thy bright and soul-filled eye,
Not for thy cheeks which with roses vie,
Not for the grace of which thou canst boast,
Not for thy beauty I love thee most, —

But for the cultured mind thou hast,
That which will beauty, yea, time outlast;
And for thy gentle and loving heart,
I love thee with love that will not depart.

WRATH.

When wrath clouds the brow, there is always
  A shadow thrown over the heart,
And Peace, with her radiant light,
  From the bosom is sure to depart.
Oh! keep then from passion and anger, —
  They bring but regret in their path;
And by being unkind, we are robbed
  Of earth's pleasure, — what little it hath.

At most, we may know but a little
  Of Eden-like pleasure and joy;
Oh! suffer not words of unkindness
  To mix with that little alloy.
It is best to treat every one kindly,
  Even those who are unkind to us;
It will melt the cold ice in their heart's core,
  And peace will be ours, doing thus.

CAN I FORGET THEE?

CAN I forget thee ? can I e'er
  Forget the blissful days of yore ?
Or can I, — can I ever teach
  My heart to worship thee no more ?
Oh, when the power shall cease, which points
  The needle to yon polar-sphere,
Then may the spell be broken too,
  Which binds my heart to thine fore'er !

Too happy were the hours we've met
  As we, alas ! shall meet no more ;
Too sweet the dreams, — which now are past,
  Too bright the hopes, — that now are o'er,

For me to cast off now the spell
  Which binds my heart to thine so fast;
Oh, when it throbs no more for thee,
  That moment 't will have throbbed its last!

But fare thee well! and I will try
  To teach my heart to do God's will;
Though Hope hath fled, forever fled,
  Thank Heaven I have *one* pleasure still;
And that, — to ever pray to Him
  Who answereth the soul's deep prayer,
To fill thy heart with happiness,
  And let not sorrow enter there!

THE SEXTON'S GRAVE.

A SEXTON dug a grave one day,
  And I was passing by;
While pausing there, I heard him say,
  "Who'll be the next to die, —
Who'll be the next one called upon
To put immortal garments on?"

He further mused, and then he said :
  "That man across the way,
Whose snowy locks o'ershade his head,
  Has little time to stay!
I think he'll be the next to die,
And slumbering in the grave to lie."

A few short days had quickly sped
  When, passing there once more,
I saw, close by, the new-made bed
  Of some one gone before.
I asked an old man standing near,
"Pray, tell me who is sleeping here?"

" Our sexton, free from care and strife,"
  The white-haired man replied;
" Though young and in the prime of life,
  Three days ago he died!
I thought not death would lay him low,
And spare these withered locks of snow!"

FOR ANNETTE'S ALBUM.

THINK not, my friend of early years,
　That time or chance can tear away
The friendship which, within my heart,
　Has rooted deeper every day.
Whatever changes fate may bring,
　Whatever be thy future lot,
Unblighted shall it flourish still,
　The frost of years can chill it not!

And many, many years from this,
　If I am wandering still below,
White-haired and near an old man's grave,
　'T will be the sweetest joy I know, —
To think of hours I've spent with thee,
　And sigh to think they are no more;
To spread my fancy's rainbow-wings,
　Fly back and live our meetings o'er!

OUR CHILDHOOD'S HOME.

THERE is a spell which binds us to the spot
Where childhood's bright and sunny years were passed;
And though we roam, that place is ne'er forgot, —
We cherish it and love it to the last.

Though duty call us from that spot to stray
Upon some other and far distant shore,
We turn from every foreign scene away,
And long to greet our childhood's home once more.

Why wonder that our fondest love should cling,
E'en to life's close, to that dear, hallowed spot?
For there we used to laugh, and sport, and sing,
And care was then a cup we tasted not.

'T was there we knew a mother's tender care,
  And friends were linked by love unto the heart
There childhood's sky was ever bright and fair,
  Or if a cloud arose, it soon was broke apart.

'T was there we roamed, to joyousness awake,
  And life seemed to us but a blissful dream;
And there a thousand things occurred, which make
  That spot the brightest isle in life's broad stream.

Oh! strong 's the spell that binds us to the spot
  Where childhood's bright and sunny years were passed;
And though we roam, that place is ne'er forgot, —
  We cherish it and love it to the last.

THE SEPARATION.

THOU who hast long been wont with me to share
   Whatever fate might pour
Into my life-cup, whether joy or care;
Thou who hast long been wont upon my breast
Thy head to pillow for repose and rest;
Thou who hast been a soothing mate, a wife,
Shedding thy smiles like sunshine on my life,—
   We part forevermore,
As part two waves that meet and break upon the shore!

Henceforth through life one path no more is ours;
   No longer side by side
We breathe the odor of the selfsame flowers;

But as the South's divided from the North,
So are our paths divided; and henceforth
My breast's no more thy pillow, and my arm
No more a shield to keep thee from all harm;
  And more, the mighty tide
Henceforth between us rolls, of passion, scorn, and pride!

Our hearts each other will repel;—as part
  Two friends that oft have met,   ~
To bear each other's image in the heart,—
To name each other in their prayers at night,
And long for days of absence to take flight,
We do not part; but striving we shall go,
Each other's image from the breast to throw;
  To bear against regret,
And, were it possible, each other to forget!

We part,—oh! mad'ning is the thought!—the leaves
  Seem from my life-book torn!
My very soul bows to the dust and grieves!
But how is it with thee? Say, in thy heart
Is there no shame, no sorrow, that we part?

No: I can read it in thy cold, stern eye;
Thy breast is but the home of perfidy!
  Alas, and yet I mourn
Not more for my poor self, than for the babe thou 'st borne!

Sweet child! it is thy sad and dreary lot,
  While thou shalt journey here,   ·
A father's loving care, to know it not;
It is thy lot to launch on life's rough tide
With no fond father to direct and guide;
To cross, perchance, the sea of destiny,
With none to tell thee where the dangers lie!
  But He who sees each tear
Of parting that I shed, — may He be ever near!

And now, my babe, oh, with what lovingness,
  Upon thy dimpled cheek,
Perchance the last, fond, yearning kiss I press!
When thou hast learned to prattle and to play,
I shall not joy to watch thy childish way;
For never more thy smile my heart shall cheer,
Thy lips may never call me " father" here!

Farewell, sweet babe! to speak
The anguish that I feel, words are too few and weak!

And thou, O false, inconstant, faithless wife,
  Whose broken love hath cast
A shameful shadow o'er my future life,
Go, go thy way, and from this parting hour,
Forget thou e'er wast mine, if thou hast power!
But ah! thou hast not, thou canst not forget;
Oft in thy dreams I shall be with thee yet;
  And the bright hours we've passed
In cloudless joy and peace will haunt thee to the last!

But go thy way! and may kind Fortune fill,
  Until it runneth o'er,
Thy cup with happiness, — I bless thee still!
But thou canst not be happy; thou wilt cast,
Too late, regretful looks upon the past;
And all thy sin and faithlessness shall bring
Deep sorrow yet thy perjured heart to wring!
  Yet would my bosom pour
A blessing on thee still;—farewell, forevermore!

HAD THAT STAR SHONE FOR ME.

DAY-STAR and guide-star of my soul,
  Which in life's morning shone so bright,
Thou wert to me, — and once I hoped
  Thou wouldst be such until the night.
But ere the morning hours were past,
  How bitterly I wept to see
The last faint ray of hope expire,
  And know that star shone not for me!

And then I said, "I must not mourn;
  Rise up, my spirit! and forget
How bright that star of morning shone;
  And oh, thou may'st be happy yet!"

And since that hour, in many lands,
  I 've sought for Lethe's fabled stream,
But memory holds its brightness still,
  And still that star shines in my dream.

I 've sought the merry revel too,
  The halls where mirth and joy control,
And mingled gayly with the gay,
  To quench this passion of my soul;
But it hath only taught me this,
  That true love knoweth no decay;
That hearts that deeply, truly love,
  Must love for aye, — must love for aye!

And now I walk alone, like one
  Whose heart is like a burial-urn,
Where all its once bright hopes repose,
  Cold ashes which no more shall burn;—
Like one who gropes his weary way
  Upon some dark, benighted lea,
Thinking how bright life might have been,
  Had that star only shone for me!

SUMMER MORNING IN THE COUNTRY.

Aurora comes! her face grows bright and brighter,
  The shades of night before her glances fly;
And in her smile the lamps of heaven grow whiter;
  Now one alone is left to gem the sky.

Delightful hour! fit time for Nature's lover
  To wander forth and talk with her alone;
To gaze upon her face and there, discover
  Her wondrous truths and make them all his own!

How soft the balmy breeze! it seemeth laden
  With all that's sweet and grateful to the sense;
To breathe the pure, fresh air, come forth, pale maiden,
  Health's rosy cheek shall be thy recompense.

The happy birds on every bough are singing
  Praise unto God who sends the morning bright;

How cheerfully the welkin's dome is ringing,
  They seem to feel a rapturous delight!

How bright the dew-refreshéd eyes of flowers,
  So softly opening to the morning's ray;
They, too, seem glad, they smile from fields and bowers,
  And unto heaven rich incense-offerings pay!

How crimson now the orient is growing;
  The sun will soon peep o'er the eastern hills;
He comes! see how the mountain-tops are glowing,
  While shadow yet the lowly valley fills!

Now in the field the mower's scythe is sounding,
  The strong-armed smith, — I hear his bellows blow;
All, all is life, and Nature's pulse is bounding,
  Which seemed so sluggish but an hour ago!

Oh! ye who dwell in the pent streets and alleys,
  Ye lose the sweetest smile that nature wears;
Leave your dark dens, — come to the hills and valleys,
  If ye would see the pomp the summer morning bears!

COME TO MY GRAVE, AND SMILE.

Oh! were I on my death-bed now,
  I think that I would say,
You must not mourn for me, dear friends,
  When I have passed away;
But when you come unto my grave
  Look up, and brightly smile,
To think that my freed spirit's gaze
  Is on you there the while!

When this poor body dies, my soul
  Will be an angel then,
And you will only bury what
  Was once my spirit's den.

Then, in the angel-form, unseen
  I still shall hover near
To bless you, and I would not see
  You shed the bitter tear.

I would not see you come and weep
  Above my lowly bed,
As though you mourned that from life's care
  And sorrow I had fled;
As though you thought that I laid there
  A prisoner in the tomb;
As though you knew not I had found
  The realms of fadeless bloom.

But rather let me see you come
  Unto my grave and smile,
To think that my freed spirit's gaze
  Is on you there the while;
To think I've crossed life's troubled sea,
  And reached that blissful shore,
Where we shall all, all meet again,
  And part — sweet thought — no more !

WEEP NOT FOR HIM.

WEEP not for him who in life's morn
  Hath from your number fled;
He was too fair and good for earth,
  Then why should tears be shed?
Think that 't is good to die in youth,
  Ere life its charm hath lost;
Ere in this cold and sinful world
  The soul is tempest-tossed.

'Tis true his pleasant, tuneful voice,
  Ye never more will hear,
And ne'er again his sunny smile
  Your sinking hearts will cheer;

Nor will those eyes of lustrous blue
  Be opened here again,
For in the quiet grave he sleeps,
  Beyond the reach of pain!

But God thought best to take him hence,
  Or he could not have died;
Remember 't was an all-wise God
  Who took him from your side.
And when thy walk is ended here,
  When this short dream is o'er,
In heavenly mansions, bright and fair,
  He 'll thy lost one restore!

Then when you go unto his grave,
  Sad, weary, and forlorn,
Remember that an angel's crown
  Doth now his brow adorn;
And weep not him who in life's morn
  Hath from your number fled,—
He was too fair and good for earth,
  Then why should tears be shed?

REQUITED LOVE.

O LOVE, if all the wealth of earth
  Could be bestowed on me,
I would not take it, if thereby
  I were forgot by thee:
For it would never give me joy
  To live in halls of gold,
If for that wealth I knew that I
  Thy priceless love had sold !.

Then say again thou 'lt love me still,
  When many years are past;
That come what will, thou wilt be true
  As long as life shall last;

That though all other friends may flee,
   Thou wilt be still the same,
And adverse winds will only serve
   To brighten up love's flame !

Thou need'st not speak,— the beaming light,
   In thy soft azure eyes,
Raised unto mine so lovingly,
   With fervency, replies,—
" O friend, my dearest earthly friend,
   Think not my love can change ;
Its holy spell within my heart
   Time never can estrange ! "

Enough! one drop of pleasure more
   My cup would overflow ;
'T is all the joy I ask, that thou
   Wilt share my lot below !
And thou shalt never rue the hour
   Thou pledged thy heart to me,—
My constant study shall be this,
   To worthy prove of thee !

THE LAKE OF YOUTH.

How beautiful in after years
The home of our lost youth appears!
And there is in each human heart
A room by Memory set apart
To hold bright pictures of that home,
When far away from it we roam!

I wander now in Memory's hall,
And look at pictures on the wall, —
Most beautiful pictures of a cot,
Which, though I roam, is ne'er forgot;
Where such bright dreams of life I dreamed,
And thought a silent lake it seemed;
Where first I· said, "How sweet to live,"
And thought not future years could give

Such beating storms,—such wrecking waves;
Such dark, dark days,—such deep, deep graves
For perished hopes; such dreadful fears—
Such lasting pain,—such burning tears!

Oh! there life *was* a silent lake,
Whose glassy surface scarce did break;
Though grief sometimes obscured the sky
To see some hope, some blossom die,
Yet on the lake's unruffled breast
I had much left to make me blest.
Ah me, I clasp an aching brow
To think I've left its bosom now!

One morn I passed into a bay—
It seemed so—which before me lay;
Alas, it was a mighty river,
And the still lake was left forever!
Now down the outlet's rushing tide,
With dangerous rocks on either side,
My boat is borne. God grant me skill,
Wisdom to steer from every ill!

Fair Lake of Como! though thy name
Is loved by poets and by fame;
Though in the evening twilight's gleam,
Or in Aurora's crimson beam,
Thy beauty, so superbly bright,
Fills the rapt artist with delight,
Fairer was that on which my oar
Shall break the level brim no more;
As much more bright as worlds where bliss
Shall end not, brighter are than this!
And when I hear the swelling roar
Of *the* Niagara before,
O'er which I know my boat must leap
Into eternity's broad deep;
When in those waters' deaf'ning sound
I hear no other tones around;
When the dark mists which there arise
Shall veil the earth-shore from my eyes,—
Oh! in that moment's awful stay,
Up life's long stream my mind will stray,
Where once the world seemed love and truth,
Upon the placid LAKE OF YOUTH!

TO A SISTER, WITH A PRESENT.

DEAR sister, take this simple gift,
    And let it ever be
A sacred relic, prized and dear,
    By which remember me.
Sometimes, perhaps, in fields of joy
    And pleasure we may reap;
But oft stern Fate will do her worst,
    And we shall mourn and weep!
But, sister dear, in after years,
    Whate'er our lot may be,
Press this memento to thy heart,
    And often think of me!

MARINTHA.

RESPECTFULLY INSCRIBED TO MR. AND MRS. J. STANNARD.

MARINTHA, from that brighter sphere,
  Where thou art dwelling now in bliss,
Canst thou look down upon us here,
  Or come unseen to visit this?
Oh, if thou canst, — if thou canst hear
  Our sighs, and all our weeping see,
Forgive, forgive each selfish tear
  That all unbidden flows for thee!

We know, — we know that thou dost roam
  Where fadeless flowers perfume the air,
That in thy bright Elysian home,
  All things are beautiful and fair;

And oh, we know bliss far more sweet
  Is thine in that celestial clime,
Than ever yet they knew whose feet
  Roamed wearily the shore of time!

But oh! how much we miss thy face
  Around the board, beside the hearth,
And it is sad to think thy place
  Will know thee here no more on earth!
Then if thou canst our sighing hear,
  And all our bitter weeping see,
Forgive, forgive each selfish tear
  That all unbidden flows for thee!

THE MAGDALEN.

Look not at her so scornfully,
  Though stained with sin and shame;
Oh, think how soft and stealthily
  The disguised Tempter came.
Think how, with all a villain's art,
  And many a subtle word,
He charmed her as the cunning snake
  Charmeth the helpless bird!

Look not at her so scornfully,
  Thy words of chiding spare;
If thou couldst ope that sin-crushed heart,
  And read the record there,

Perchance far whiter than thou think'st
　Those pages would appear,
And thou wouldst change that look of scorn
　Into a pitying tear!

Look not at her so scornfully,
　And say, "a Magdalen;"
God can forgive the blackest sin,
　And so should " Christian " men!
But help her with thy hand to rise,
　For oh, the world's cold frown,
Thou canst not know how heavily
　It holds the fallen down!

Look not at her so scornfully,
　For it is not for thee
To judge how darkly stained by sin
　Another's heart may be.
Oh, those who have in weakness erred,
　Look kindly still at them,
And He who can their bosoms read,
　Let Him alone condemn!

PARTING WORDS.

When loved ones lie upon the bed of death,
  About to pass from earthly scenes away,
About to close this life of mortal breath,
  What words of parting shall we speak, — oh, say?

Oh, in that hour of grief, what words can tell
  The parting wish the breaking heart would speak!
The fond "good-by," the passionate "farewell,"
  When heard beside the dying bed, how weak!

Then breathe them never unto one whose sight
  Hath caught the shining of the spires above;
But whisper, if the lips can speak, "Good-night!
  'T is close of life's short day, good-night, my love!

"And oh! beloved, this night will bring a morn,—
  One brighter far than thou hast seen below;
Our Father's smile will everything adorn,
  We would not keep thee here, good-night, love, go!

" And when o'er us, too, falls the night of life,—
  When o'er Eternity's white hills we greet
The morning's beams, far from this mortal strife,
  Earth's care and pain, how will we fly to meet!

" Then will God's smile dry all our tears away,
  As sunbeams dry a flower that 's wet with dew;
And Death shall part us there no more for aye,—
  No more shall Sorrow in our track pursue!

" Gently as flowers at morning hour unfold,
  Fall now the curtain o'er thy earthly sight;—
What splendor will thy spirit-eyes behold,
  So soon to ope!—good-night, beloved, good-night!"

WILT THOU REMEMBER ME?

WE part, — but oh, the blissful hours
  Thy side I've lingered near,
Till life's last, feeble beat is o'er,
  Will be to memory dear!
Nor can this heart of mine forget
  How oft at close of day,
It hath thrilled to hear thy silver voice,
  Poured forth in some sweet lay!

And say, dear one, when years have fled,
  And at some twilight hour,
Dreams of the past come o'er thy mind
  With sweet and magic power;
Or when, upon the evening air,
  Thy songs float clear and free,
As when we met in days gone by,
  Wilt thou remember me?

STANZA.

Oh, seldom express your love in words,
  For their power is all too weak,
And the eye hath a better and softer way,
  The language of love to speak!